No, Magoo.
This is for you.

No, Magoo.
This is for you.

Can't get in.
Claw my way through?

**No, Magoo.
This is for you.**

Mouth is dry.
This drink tastes ...blue?

No! Magoo!

# THIS
## is for you.

Oooh, mud bath!

squish

squash

wahoooooo

No, Magoo.
This is for you.

What? For me?
It can't be true ...

Yes, Magoo!